Wish Again, Big Bear

By
Richard J. Margolis

Pictures by
Robert Lopshire

THE MACMILLAN COMPANY
New York, New York

The Macmillan Company, 866 Third Avenue, New York, N. Y. 10022
Collier-Macmillan Canada Ltd., Toronto, Ontario

Library of Congress catalog card number: 75-160070
Printed in the United States of America

10 9 8 7 6 5 4 3 2 1

The three-color illustrations are pen-and-ink line drawings
with overlays on acetate for brown and green. The type face
is Century Schoolbook.

To my mother,
who gave me
the words

Big Bear caught a fish.

The fish was shiny and very upset.

"There's been a mistake,

there's been a mistake,"

Fish yelled, flipping and flopping

in Big Bear's net.

"I don't think so,"
Big Bear said politely.
"You're just what I want for lunch."

Fish thought fast.

"Nonsense!" he said.

"Don't you know I'm a wish-fish?
Instead of eating me you should
ask me to grant you three wishes.
That's what wish-fish do—
they grant wishes."

"Oh," Big Bear said.

"I never knew that before."

"Well you know it now,"
  Fish said, coughing and gasping.
"Now hurry up and
  make your three wishes.
  I'm drowning in all this air."

Big Bear dropped Fish
into a pail of water.
"If I told you my first wish,"
he said, "you might laugh."

"Not a chance," said Fish.

"We wish-fish hear all kinds of
funny wishes, but we never laugh."

"Are you sure?"

"Positive."

"Well then," said Big Bear,
"I wish ... I wish ...
I wish I could be more *graceful*."

Fish laughed.

He laughed so hard
he filled the pail with bubbles.

Big Bear sighed.

"I knew you'd laugh," he said.

"Maybe I should just eat you
and be done with it."

"Let's not be hasty," Fish said.

"Your wish is granted. I'll make
you graceful in a jiffy."

Fish spread his fins, stood up
on his tail and chanted:
    "Let Big Bear dance
    Let Big Bear prance
    Let Big Bear chase
    the bird of grace."

"Ok," said Fish,

"now you're graceful."

"I am?" said Big Bear.

"Sure you are," said Fish.

"Do a dance."

Big Bear began to dance.

The earth shook.

"What style!" said Fish.

"What grace!"

Big Bear tripped over a rock

and fell on his face.

"Beautiful," said Fish.

"A delight to the eyes."

Big Bear twirled twice

and knocked down an oak tree.

"I'm graceful, I'm graceful,"

he shouted. "How grateful I am

to be graceful."

"It was nothing," Fish said.

"Just throw me back in the pond."

"You promised me two more wishes,"

said Big Bear, waltzing into

a blueberry bush.

"Ok, ok," Fish said.

"Throw me another wish."

Big Bear sat down.

"If I told you my second wish,"
he said, "you might laugh again."

"No, I really wouldn't,"
Fish said. "I'm a wish-fish,
and we wish-fish never laugh."

"Promise?"

"Cross my heart and
hope to live," said Fish.

"Well then," said Big Bear,
"I wish . . .
I wish I could be SMALL!"
Fish laughed.
He laughed so hard
the pail almost tipped over.

Big Bear put a paw on the pail.

"I'm hungry," he said.

"Your wish is granted,"
said Fish hastily.

"I'll make you small
in no time at all."

Fish leaned over the rim
of the pail and sang:
    "Bear brawn
      Be gone
      before next dawn.
    Think small
    Shrink all."

"Ok," said Fish,

"now you're small."

"I am?" said Big Bear.

"Sure. Try hiding and you'll see."

Fish covered his eyes with his fins

and counted to ten.

Big Bear ran to a low bush and
hid behind it.

"Here I come, ready or not,"
Fish called. Fish put his fins down.
He saw Big Bear right away.

"Now where could that dinky bear
have gone to?" Fish said, looking
all around. "Where, oh where,
is tiny Big Bear?"

"I'm over here," Big Bear called.
"I'm hiding behind this little bush."

Fish clapped his fins.

"Well that beats all," he said.

"I looked right at that bush
and didn't even see you.
You've lost weight, Big Bear."

"I'm small, I'm small,"
Big Bear shouted.

"I'm so happy to be small."

"Don't give it another thought,"
said Fish. "Just throw me back
in the pond."

Big Bear pulled the bush out of the
ground and used it to fan himself.

"I hate to seem ungrateful," he said,
"but you owe me one more wish."
"You're right," Fish said.
"Wish away."
"You're going to laugh again,
  aren't you?" said Big Bear.
"No," said Fish, "I think not."

"It's a pretty hard wish,"
Big Bear said. "But I guess
it never hurts to ask."
"Sometimes it hurts," said Fish.
"You'll know when you've asked."

"Well," said Big Bear,

"I wish . . . I wish . . .

well, I wish I had a friend."

Fish did not laugh.

"I'm not sure I can do that

for you, Big Bear," he said.

"Making a friend takes

a lot of magic."

"Even when a fellow's small

and graceful?" Big Bear asked.

"Even when a fellow's small

and graceful," Fish answered.

They were silent for a long time.
Then Fish said: "Big Bear, you
can go ahead and eat me now.
You didn't get your three wishes,
and a bargain's a bargain."
"Yes," said Big Bear.
"I guess that's true.
A bargain's a bargain."

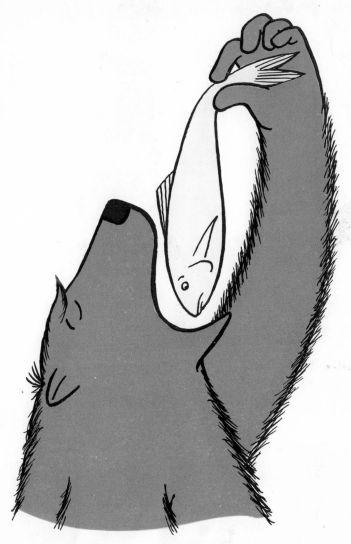

Big Bear grabbed Fish by the tail.
Then he opened his mouth
very wide.

"Goodby, Fish," said Big Bear.

"Goodby, Big Bear," said Fish.

"I'll miss you, Fish."

"I'll miss *you*, Big Bear."

"We had some good times together,
didn't we, Fish?"

"Indeed we did, Big Bear."

"Fish? ... "

"What is it, Big Bear?"

"I can't eat you, Fish. It's hard
to eat somebody you know."

Fish laughed.

He laughed so hard that he fell
right out of Big Bear's paw
and landed back in the pond.
Big Bear sniffled.
"You're laughing because
you tricked me," he said.

"No," said Fish.
"I'm laughing because your
third wish has come true."

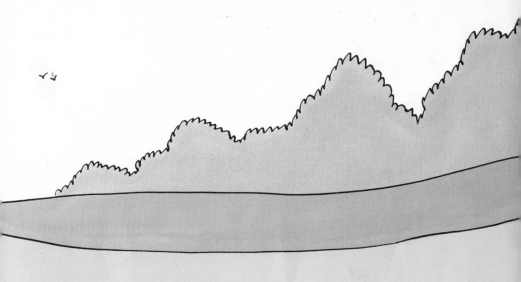

And the two
were friends forevermore.

RICHARD J. MARGOLIS's stories and poems for children include *The Upside-Down King*, *Looking for a Place*, and *Only the Moon and Me*. A freelance writer, he has contributed articles and reviews to *The New York Times*, *Life*, *The New Leader*, and many other publications.

Mr. Margolis lives in Connecticut with his wife, Diane, and his two sons, Harry and Philip.

ROBERT LOPSHIRE is the author and illustrator of *Put Me in the Zoo, How to Make Flibbers, I Am Better Than You, It's Magic?* and other fun-to-read books. He and his family live in Cochranville, Pennsylvania.